G.P. Putnam's Sons • New York

Copyright © 1998 by Eric Hill.
All rights reserved. This book, or parts thereof, may not be reproduced in any form without
permission in writing from the publisher, G. P. Putnam's Sons,
a division of The Putnam & Grosset Group, 200 Madison Avenue, New York, NY 10016.
G. P. Putnam's Sons, Reg. U.S. Pat. & Tm. Off.
Planned and produced by Ventura Publishing Ltd.,
27 Wrights Lane, London W8 5TZ, England.
Published simultaneously in Canada.
Printed and bound in Singapore by Tien Wah Press (Pte) Ltd.
L.C. number 97-69068. ISBN 0-399-23222-2
1 3 5 7 9 10 8 6 4 2

Spot and his Grandparents
Go to the Carnival

Eric Hill

Spot is going to visit his grandparents. He waves good bye to his mom, Sally, and his dad, Sam, and runs across the field to Grandma and Grandpa's house. Spot is excited. He's going to the carnival with Grandma and Grandpa.

Spot rings the doorbell and Kitty runs away. She doesn't like loud noises. Grandpa opens the door. He acts surprised to see Spot.

"Hello, Spot!" he says. "What are you doing here?"

"Oh, Grandpa!" Spot says. "You know! We're going to the carnival today!"

"Of course we are, Spot," Grandpa says, laughing. He gives Spot a big hug. "Grandma and I are getting everything ready. Come up to the attic and see."

Spot likes going to the attic. Grandma and Grandpa keep all the things they can't fit into the rest of the house—chairs and chests full of things, clothes, toys, pictures and lots of boxes.

Grandma is sorting out the decorations.

"Hello, Grandma! Can I help?" Spot asks.

"Why, thank you, Spot," Grandma says. "My, goodness, you're having fun with those boxes. What have you found under there?"

"A fire fighter's helmet!" Spot says.

"That's mine," Grandpa says.

"Were you really a fire fighter, Grandpa?" Spot asks.

"Your grandpa wasn't just a fire fighter," Grandma tells Spot. "He was the Chief!"

"That reminds me," Grandpa says. "I've got a surprise for you. Let's go and see."

Grandpa is very good at surprises. They go down the stairs and into the garden.

Grandpa tells Spot to stand in front of the shed and close his eyes. Spot hears the sound of the shed doors opening.
"You can look now, Spot."

Spot sees the most wonderful sight. A bright red fire engine with a long ladder and a big brass bell.

"Grandpa! Is it really yours?"
"This is the fire engine I used to work on. The fire fighters have a new one now, so I'm looking after this one. It just needs cleaning before we use it in the parade going to the carnival."

"The parade! You mean we're going to be in the parade on the fire engine? Oh, my friends should see this!"
"But they can come with us, Spot, and be our crew," Grandpa says.
Spot telephones his friends right away.

While Spot waits for Helen, Tom and Steve to arrive, he helps Grandpa clean the fire engine. Grandpa gets a little wet.

"Spot," Grandma calls out, "your friends are here!"
  Spot finds them in the kitchen eating cookies.
  "Your grandma's cookies are fantastic!" Tom says.
  "Yes, they are," Spot says, "and you should taste
Grandma's cake. Every year Grandma wins the prize
for the best cake at the carnival!"

"Let's go see Grandpa's fire engine," Spot says.
They all run out to the shed.
   "Wow!" Tom says.
   "Gosh!" Helen says. Steve just stares.
   "Climb aboard," Grandpa tells them.

Spot rings the brass bell.
"Ding, ding!"

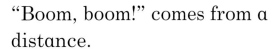

"Boom, boom!" comes from a distance.

"What's that?" Steve asks.

"Don't know," everyone says.

"Ding, ding, ding!" Spot rings the bell.

"Boom, boom, boom," comes the answer.

"It sounds like a drum," Spot says. "Let's go and look."

They run down to the garden gate. A gaily decorated float passes by. On the back are a bear with a drum, an elephant with a trumpet, and a hippo with a tuba.

"That's my mom. She plays the tuba. Where are you going, Mom?" Helen shouts.

"We're on our way to pick up the rest of the band. Do you want to look at our float?"

Tom and Steve like the musical instruments. Tom taps the drum. "Boom, boom." Steve blows into the tuba. "Screech, screech!"
   The loud noises scare Kitty. She runs up a tree and hides.

Grandma comes to tell them it's time to go
to the parade. "Have you seen Kitty?" she asks.
"She's up the tree," Spot tells Grandma.
Grandma gets a saucer of milk and calls to Kitty.
But she won't come down. She's too scared.
"Kitty's stuck," Helen says.

Steve is good at climbing trees.
"I'll get her," he says.

He reaches Kitty and sits next to her.
"I can't carry her," he shouts down.
"I need my arms to hold Kitty and I need
them to climb down the tree. I can't do both.
I'll just stay here and keep Kitty company until
help comes."

The fire engine bounces down the path with Grandma at the wheel and Grandpa on the ladder. It stops next to the tree.

"Quick, put the ladder up, Grandpa!" Grandma says.

"I can't until Spot gets here," Grandpa says.

Just then Spot runs out of the house with Grandpa's fire fighter's helmet. "Now I'm ready for anything," Grandpa says, putting on the helmet.

Slowly the ladder goes up, higher and higher. It reaches the branch where Kitty and Steve are sitting. Grandpa climbs up and rescues Kitty. Steve comes down the ladder after them.

Everyone cheers. "Well done, everyone!" Grandma says. "Now we can go to the parade."

"Ding, ding!" They are off. Grandma is wearing her helmet.

"You look like a real fire fighter now," Spot says.

"She was," Grandpa says. "We were a great team."

"We still are," Grandma says with a smile.

Suddenly around a corner, they come upon a sad sight. A float is parked at the side of the road. It has a very flat back tire.

"Mom," Helen says, "you have a flat tire!"

"We certainly do," Helen's mom says. "Do you have a spare tire you can lend us to get to the parade?"

"Our spare is the wrong size," Grandpa says.

"Oh, dear," Helen's mom says.

"I have an idea, Grandpa," Spot says and whispers in his ear.

"That *is* a good idea, Spot!"

The band gets to ride in the parade, but not on their own float. Thanks to Spot they join the parade on Grandpa's fire engine.

And what a parade it is! All the houses along the street are decorated with flags and banners and streamers.

People laugh and cheer as clowns, jugglers, acrobats pass by with the floats.

"Look, Grandma! Look, Grandpa! There's Mom and Dad!" Spot shouts. Sally and Sam wave proudly at the fire engine. Spot waves back and rings the bell as loudly as he can. Just as they enter the carnival grounds, balloons fly up into the sky and the parade is covered with shiny balloons.

When it's all over, Spot thinks it is the best carnival day ever.

"It was wonderful riding on the fire engine," he says.

"And Grandma won first prize for the best cake again!" Grandpa says proudly.

"Spot, you should have the blue ribbon this year because you rescued the band and saved the day!" Grandma says.

Spot takes the blue ribbon and pins it on the wall. "Let's keep it here with all the others," he says. "I think we all saved the day!"